BEST FRIENDS

Pat L Sargent

TACE SARGENT

10 13 2000

BEST FRIENDS

Dave Sargent

Illustrated by
Blaine Sapaugh

Ozark Publishing, Inc.
P.O. Box 389
Redfield, Arkansas 72132

F
Sar   Sargent, Dave
        Best Friends, by Dave Sargent. Illus. by Blaine
        Sapaugh.
        Ozark Publishing, Inc., 1993.
        40P. illus.
        Summary: A boy and his dog and their life
        together.
        1. Dogs. I. Title.

ISBN Casebound-1-56763-056-1
ISBN Paperback-1-56763-057-X

Ozark Publishing, Inc.
P.O. Box 389, 439 Rhoads Rd.
Redfield, AR 72132
Ph: 1-800-321-5671

Printed in the United States of America

INSPIRED BY

My old dog and my best friend Tippy.

DEDICATED TO

Trevor Ruiz, my grandson.

FOREWORD

Johnny and Sparky grew up together and they were best friends.

When Johnny was four years old, a

little puppy came to his house one day.

When Johnny was five, the puppy
was full grown. Johnny named him

4

Sparky, and Sparky played with Johnny all the time.

W hen Johnny was six, he started
to school. Sparky went to school with

Johnny every day and waited by the
door until school was out so he could
walk Johnny home.

W hen Johnny was seven, he got a little red wagon for his birthday.

Sparky pulled the little red wagon all around while Johnny rode.

When Johnny was eight, he got a new skateboard, and Sparky pulled

the skateboard up and down the side-
walk while Johnny rode.

When Johnny was nine, he went camping with the Boy Scouts.

Sparky went with him and protected him from all the wild animals.

When Johnny was ten, he played baseball all the time. Sparky would

fetch all the stray balls and bring
them back to Johnny.

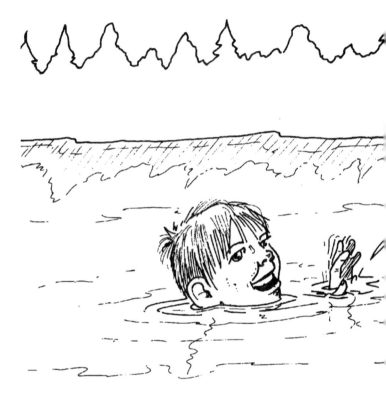

When Johnny was eleven, he loved to swim in the creek. Sparky was always

there for Johnny and once saved him
from drowning.

When Johnny was twelve, he loved
to hike in the woods and fish in the

nearby stream. Sparky was always there
with him to protect him from the snakes.

When Johnny was thirteen, he didn't want Sparky around anymore.

He went places where dogs couldn't go
and did things that dogs couldn't do.

When Johnny was fourteen,
Sparky was getting old, and Johnny

made him stay in the house all the time.

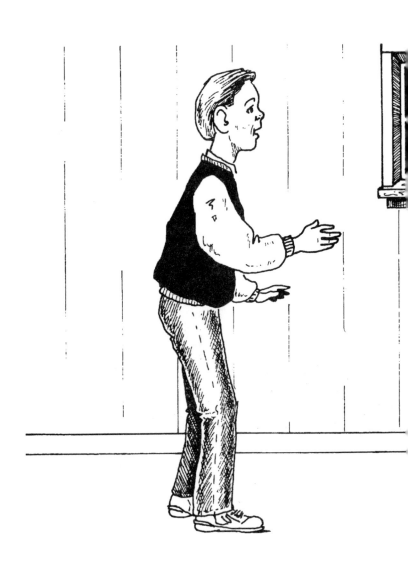

When Johnny was fifteen, he came
home one day to find the veterinarian
with Sparky. He asked, "Doctor, what's

wrong with Sparky?" The doctor said,
"Your dog is dying from old age and
loneliness."

Johnny knelt on the floor beside Sparky and said, "I'm sorry, Sparky, for leaving you alone so much."

Sparky looked at Johnny as if to say,
"It's okay, Johnny. I love you anyway."

The doctor handed Johnny some
vitamins and said, "Give your dog

one of these vitamins every day. It will make him feel better."

The doctor opened the door and walked outside. Then he turned back and added, "The best medicine you can give your dog is love. I would bet

my last dollar that you and the dog have
had some good times together." Tears
came to Johnny's eyes as he smiled and
nodded.

Sparky was lying on his rug in the utility room. He had been sleeping

there ever since Johnny had gotten too
big and too busy to play with him.

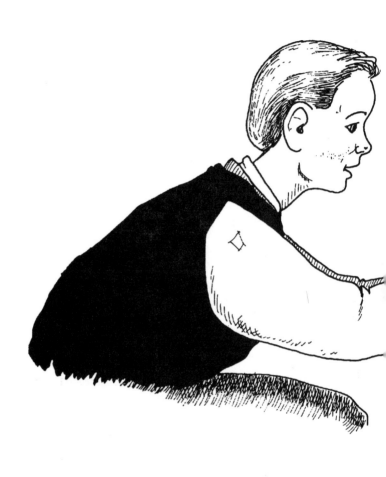

J ohnny knelt down beside Sparky and took his head in his hands. He looked deep into Sparky's eyes and with a

quivering voice said, "I'm moving you back into my room, Sparky. I'm going to take real good care of you."

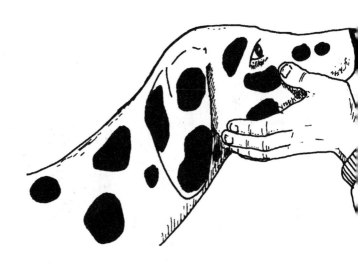

Sparky's eyes took on a glow again as he watched Johnny's face and listened to Johnny's voice. There was something in Johnny's voice that he recognized.

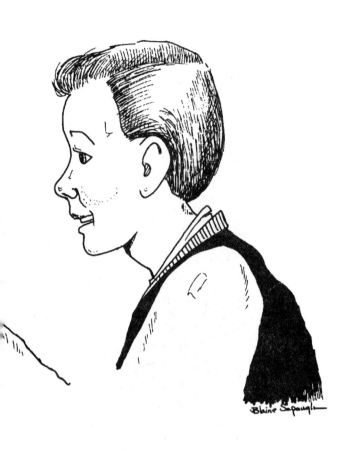

It was something that he hadn't heard
in a long, long time; it was a warm and
caring sound. It was the sound of love.

Sparky whined a low whine and licked Johnny's salty face; the salt was from the tears on Johnny's cheeks. Easing his hands under Sparky,

Blaine Sapaugh

Johnny gently picked him up and carried him to his room–the room they had shared since they were very small.

Sparky closed his eyes and only min-
utes later was dreaming of a trickling
stream and a small boy with a fishing
pole, yelling, "I got one, Sparky! I got a
big one!"